Hi! I'm Eddie.
Eddie Carlson.

This is a story about me
and my three best friends
– Haggis, Fiend and Norman.
They're monsters.

That's right. **Monsters**. Big hairy
critters with fangs and horns
and extra eyes.

They were living in the basement of
the house my family moved into.
Don't tell anyone, will you?
They're a secret. Only me, my parents
and my big sister Angela
know about them.
And it isn't easy keeping
it that way . . .

Eddie

With special thanks to
Richard Dungworth

For more monster mess and chaos,
try reading:
Me & My Monsters: Monster School

Me & My
MONSTERS ™

Monsters
in the
Basement!

RORY GROWLER

PUFFIN

PUFFIN BOOKS

Published by the Penguin Group
Penguin Books Ltd, 80 Strand, London WC2R 0RL, England
Penguin Group (USA) Inc., 375 Hudson Street, New York, New York 10014, USA
Penguin Group (Canada), 90 Eglinton Avenue East,
Suite 700, Toronto, Ontario, Canada M4P 2Y3
(a division of Pearson Penguin Canada Inc.)
Penguin Ireland, 25 St Stephen's Green, Dublin 2, Ireland
(a division of Penguin Books Ltd)
Penguin Group (Australia), 250 Camberwell Road, Camberwell, Victoria 3124, Australia
(a division of Pearson Australia Group Pty Ltd)
Penguin Books India Pvt Ltd, 11 Community Centre,
Panchsheel Park, New Delhi – 110 017, India
Penguin Group (NZ), 67 Apollo Drive, Rosedale, Auckland 0632, New Zealand
(a division of Pearson New Zealand Ltd)
Penguin Books (South Africa) (Pty) Ltd, 24 Sturdee Avenue,
Rosebank, Johannesburg 2196, South Africa

Penguin Books Ltd, Registered Offices: 80 Strand, London WC2R 0RL, England

puffinbooks.com

First published 2011
2

Copyright © Tiger Aspect Productions/The Jim Henson Company/Sticky Pictures Pty Ltd 2011
Me & My Monsters ™ & © Tiger Aspect Productions/The Jim Henson Company/
Sticky Pictures Pty Ltd 2011
Me & My Monsters is produced by Tiger Aspect Productions, The Jim Henson Company
and Sticky Pictures Pty Ltd
All rights reserved

Set in Futura Standard
Printed in Great Britain by Clays Ltd, St Ives plc

British Library Cataloguing in Publication Data
A CIP catalogue record for this book is available from the British Library

ISBN: 978–0–141–33631–2

Can You Keep a Secret?

When we moved back to England, I set my heart on getting a dog. I already have a sister, but she doesn't come when I whistle, or play fetch.

My parents said they'd think about it, which means a big fat no.

But I'm not bothered about a dog any more. Because now I've got something better. Way better.

My very own monsters.

That's right. **Monsters.** Big hairy guys with fangs and horns and extra eyes.

They were living in the basement of the house we moved into.

I'm not sure how long they'd been there. Quite a while, I think.

Here's a picture of them, so you know who's who:

FIEND

crazy multiple eyeballs

never stops talking!

full of (bad) ideas!

NORMAN

purple fur

big sticky-out nose

doesn't talk, but likes
making weird noises

HAGGIS

whopping monster
body

wicked horns

mega
mouth

(he's a big softy really)

I was the only one who knew about the monsters. I thought it might be a good idea to keep it that way.

I mean, what would *your* parents do if they found out they had monsters living in the basement? I knew mine would have a total meltdown. And there was no way I was going to introduce my new friends to my big sister Angela. For their sake!

So I decided to keep them a secret. I knew it wasn't going to be easy. I figured the first ten years would be the hardest.

As it turned out, things got tricky a lot sooner than that . . .

Lemon Bombshells

It all started with the Lemon Bombshells.
Have you ever had one? They're
amazing. The most lemony sweets ever.
And when the sherbet in the middle
kicks in . . . mmmm . . . **fizz-tastic**!
I thought Fiend, Haggis and Norman
might like to try them. So I sneaked a
few from the family sweet jar and took
them down to the basement.

They *loved* them.

'Woo-hoo!' whooped Fiend as
the sherbet explosion went off in his
monster mouth. His eyes were spinning
madly. All nine of them.

'waaaaaaah!'

yelled Haggis. His great big furry body
was shaking all over from the fizz
attack.

As for Norman – he was howling like a siren and had smoke shooting from his ears.

'Whoa! Those sweets really hit the spot!' raved Fiend. 'I've got to have another!'

'Yeah!' boomed Haggis.

'Gimme gimme gimme!'

I could tell Norman was keen, too. He didn't say anything, he never does. But he made one of his weird noises and held out his hand for another.

There was just

one problem. I only had one Bombshell left.

'One *million*?' asked Fiend.

'No,' I told him. 'One.'

'One *thousand*?' he said hopefully.

'No. Just one!'

They were silent while the news sank in. Not for long, though.

'That bad boy is *mine*!' yelled Fiend.

But the others weren't having it. They started arguing over who should get the last Bombshell.

I sighed. There was only one fair way to settle things. I'd have to have it.

'No! No! No!' pleaded Haggis as I unwrapped it. I popped it in my mouth.

'Arghh!' wailed Fiend. 'Whatever

happened to caring and sharing?'

I did feel a bit mean. They were

desperate for more Bombshells. And I

couldn't blame them. Like I said, those

sweets are *fizz-tastic*.

'I'll have to go and ask Mum,' I

told them. Mum is Guardian of the

Family Sweet Jar. Unfortunately.

13

'Do you want *us* to have a word with the upstairs human thingy people?' suggested Fiend helpfully. You have to watch out for Fiend's 'helpful' ideas.

'No!' I said quickly. 'You three stay here. My parents will throw a fit if they discover monsters are in the basement.'

'Monsters?' cried Haggis. '*Where*?' He looked around in a panic.

I left Fiend to explain that I meant *them* and set off upstairs, ready to tackle Mission Lemon Bombshell alone . . .

The Sweet Police

To get my hands on more Lemon
Bombshells, I was going to have to get
past Mum. The sweet jar was in the
kitchen – and so was she. She was
busy unpacking some of the boxes from
the move. I thought I could sneak a few
Bombshells without her noticing . . .

'Eddie Carlson!'

She'd caught me with my hand in
the jar. Rats.

'You've had enough of those for
one day,' said Mum.

'Not true!' I protested. 'I can
eat *loads* more. And I'm willing to
prove it.'

Mum gave me one of those looks. You know the kind.

'Nice try,' she said. 'But the Sweet Police say no.'

I thought it might be worth trying to negotiate a bit.

'OK. I'll just take . . . three.'

I made a break for the door, but Mum was too fast. She got me in a bear hug.

'Right! You're under arrest! You're coming to the station!'

Mum fooled around wrestling for a bit, until the sweet jar was well out of my reach.

'By the way, Eddie,' she said suspiciously. 'Have you taken my cookbooks?'

Monsters in the Basement

Mum is a great cook. In fact, she works as a chef. So no one is allowed to mess with her recipe books.

'No,' I said. 'I'm allergic to books.'

I hadn't taken them, it was true. But

I had a bad feeling I knew who had.

Of course, it turned out that Fiend, Haggis and Norman were sitting in the hall surrounded by a whole bunch of cookbooks. All three of them had a recipe book open in their monster mitts. They were flicking through the pages, looking greedily at the tasty-looking photographs.

'Ahhh! The food looks delicious!' said Fiend, casting a greedy eye – or rather, nine greedy eyes – over a selection of main courses. 'I'll say!' agreed

Haggis happily. His insides made a loud rumbling noise as he gazed hungrily at an appetizing picture.

Norman honked his agreement.

Suddenly, Fiend stopped flicking and ripped out a page from his book.

'Mmmm! I'm having the chicken fricassee with asparagus!'

Haggis had also made up his tiny mind about what his not-so-tiny stomach wanted most. He tore out his favourite food photo.

'And I'm having the lamb chops, mashed potatoes and gravy!' he said, smacking his huge lips.

Norman made a happy squealing noise as he tore out his choice of main course. A picture of some measuring spoons.

'*Bon appetit!*' cried Fiend.

All three monsters screwed up their cookbook pictures, stuffed them into their mouths and began blissfully munching away.

'Mmmmm!' mumbled Haggis. 'And it tastes as good as it looks!'

I guess they would have moved on to a second course, if they'd had the chance. But before any of them could choose pudding, there was a sound of keys jangling. A shadow appeared behind the window of the front door.

Dad was home.

Dad Gets Spooked

I don't know how the guys managed to hide themselves in time. It is one of their best talents. They have this odd way of being able to blend in with the background in the blink of an eye.

It shouldn't be possible, when you think how odd-looking they all are. And how *massive* Haggis is. It's like they were *made* to be noticed. But somehow all three of them can vanish, just like that. I don't mean they turn invisible or anything. But they can hide inside, behind, or under things in a split second. And something about the *way* they hide tricks your brain into not noticing them.

They must have pulled their disappearing act again this time, because Dad made it through the door, down the hall and into the kitchen without seeing them. Or at least without *properly* seeing them. He had some idea that he wasn't alone, though. Because when he came into the kitchen, the first thing he said to Mum was:

'Kate, do you sense a strange presence in this house?'

Mum is used to Dad being a bit stressed. She's a lot more laid-back about stuff.

'Nick!' she said. 'That's no way to talk about our children!'

But Dad wasn't in a joking mood. He was looking quite spooked.

'I just get this feeling we're not alone,' he said.

'I know. There are two of them,' said Mum, still teasing. 'Eddie and Angela.'

As they were talking, I realized this was my chance! Maybe Mission Lemon Bombshell didn't have to be a total washout after all. I quietly raided the sweet jar while Mum was talking to Dad.

'Every time I'm in this house,' Dad was saying, 'I feel like I'm being watched.'

Of course, I knew the *real* reason he felt like that. Fiend was hiding in the kitchen bin. His nine freaky eyeballs were peering out at Dad from under the lid. I gave him my best *Get out of here!* stare. He grinned at me and disappeared back into the bin.

Thankfully, my parents hadn't noticed. Mum was trying to calm Dad down. 'Sweetie,' she said, 'you've been under a lot of strain lately, with the new job and the house move.'

'Yeah, Dad,' I said. 'Maybe your mind has snapped.'

Dad gave me a look.

'My mind is fine.'

Angela came into the kitchen. For once, I was almost pleased to see her. Maybe we could get off the 'strange presence in the house' subject.

But my sister only made things worse.

As usual.

My Annoying Big Sister

'Which part of England have we moved to?' Angela asked my parents. 'Is it Spook Hill?'

It sounded like something had freaked *her* out, too. That was all I needed.

'Look,' said Mum, trying to calm everyone down. 'I know there've been a lot of odd things happening lately. But I'm sure there's a perfectly rational explanation.'

Don't be so sure, Mum, I thought. There was nothing rational about Haggis, Fiend and Norman. Especially Norman.

Angela didn't look convinced. 'Stuff is going missing from my room,' she said grumpily. 'First my iPod and now my hair-straighteners.'

Ouch. Hair stuff is a big deal for my sister.

'Maybe you just misplaced them?' suggested Mum.

Angela gave her an *I don't think so* look.

'They were in my hand at the time!' she said.

Mum didn't have an explanation for that. I did.

So I thought I'd better come up with another one.

'Maybe . . . we've got a rodent!' I suggested.

Angela raised her eyebrows.
'A mouse having a bad hair day?'

'Anything is possible,' said Mum.

My sister didn't look impressed. She
never is.

'Well, if you see one with a fancy
hairdo,' she snapped, 'kick his butt!'

And she stomped out of the kitchen.

I thought it was high time I made
myself scarce, too. I'd been distracted
from my Mission for long enough. But
Mum blocked me before I could make
it to the door.

'Not so fast!' She held out her
hand, back in Sweet Police mode. 'Let's
be having them!'

I tried to look innocent, but she
wasn't buying it. I had no choice.

I turned out my pockets and handed over the Bombshells.

Mum gave me a hard stare.

'*All* of them.'

I untucked my shirt and gave her the ones I'd hidden there.

Mum still wasn't through.

'What about the shoe?'

I took off my shoe and emptied out the last of the Bombshells. Man, she's good. She'd got the lot. As I left the kitchen, she was doing a smug little victory dance.

Does *your* mum have eyes in the back of her head, like Fiend, or is it just mine?

Panic Attack

Back down in the basement, Fiend was waiting for me.

'Did you get the Lemon Bombshells?' he demanded as soon as he saw me coming down the steps.

Haggis was with him.

'Did you, Eddie? Did you? **Didyoudidyoudidyou?**'

'I'm sorry,' I said, shaking my head. 'I tried.'

From the way the two of them reacted, you'd have thought the world had ended.

'**Noooohhh!**' wailed Fiend. 'You failed on the most *important* mission of your *life*!'

Norman popped up from nowhere
to join in the wailing. He was looking
even weirder than usual – thanks
to some odd new hat. It took me a
moment to realize what he'd got on.

'Norman,' I said. 'Why are you
wearing a pair of my *dad's underpants*
on your head?'

Norman made a mewing noise.

'He's a trendsetter,' Fiend said
simply. 'Where he leads, others follow.'

But talking to them about my dad's
underpants was going to have to wait.
'You know you shouldn't
go upstairs!' I said, trying
not to sound bossy
(I know how
annoying it is when

Angela tells me what to do). 'You could've been spotted.'

Fiend gave me a funny look. They're the sort he does best.

'We're **monsters**,' he said waving his arms. 'We're not very big on the whole *discipline* thing.'

Like I needed telling.

'And you've got to stop taking things!' I pleaded.

Angela's iPod and hair-straighteners weren't the only things that had 'gone missing' since we moved in. The basement was crammed with stuff that Fiend, Haggis and Norman – particularly Norman – had pinched. Not just from my family, but from families who lived here before us, too.

If things kept on vanishing, it was only a matter of time before my folks would be on to them.

'My parents are getting seriously suspicious,' I told them. 'If they find out about you, they'll make you all leave!'

Haggis's face fell.

'What are you saying?' he asked in a small voice. 'They won't like me?'

I looked at him, trying to be stern.

'Because I need to be loved!' he said. 'I can't handle rejection!'

Fiend wasn't nearly so bothered. 'Me, I've got nothing to worry about,' he said happily. 'I'm *adorable*. It's the eyes, you see. Who could resist?'

I couldn't help thinking that creatures with nine eyes don't

34

appear in many people's Top Ten Cute Things. But I didn't say so.

Poor old Haggis had got himself in a real state. He couldn't deal with the idea of not being liked. He'd started shaking and was breathing way too fast.

'I'm having a panic attack!' he wailed.

'oooooh! Panic attaaaaack!'

'Listen,' I said quickly, 'I'm a big monster fan. Huge! I think you guys are the best.'

This seemed to help. Haggis's furry face looked a bit less miserable and he started breathing normally again. I'd meant every word of it, too. Now for the hard part. I chose my words carefully.

'It's just that grown-ups see the world . . . *differently,*' I explained. I looked at Norman, with my dad's pants on his head. Even grown-ups didn't see things as differently as Norman did.

'For example,' I told them, 'my mum and dad really like *peace and quiet.*'

'QUIET?' yelled Fiend, getting excited. 'We can do that! I mean, we've never actually *tried*. But how hard can it be?'

For Fiend, very hard, I guessed. He was a world-class, non-stop chatterbox. He never shuts up. I couldn't even *imagine* him being quiet.

But right now he seemed determined to give it a go.

The Big Hush

'OK. Here we go,' said Fiend to Haggis and Norman. 'Zip it up. Put a sock in it. Turn the volume *waaaay* down low,' he chattered.

'Here comes the Big HUSH! In a moment, you won't be able to hear a sound. Not a thing. Not a peep! The silence will be deafening!'

There was a pause, then –

'DEAFENING, I TELLS YOU!'

I sighed. 'You're not very good at this, are you, Fiend?' I said.

Fiend looked hurt. 'Hmph! Well, aren't you the picky one?'

I turned to Norman. 'But I thought *you* did quite well.'

'He never speaks!' Fiend shouted.

'And I was impressed with you, too,' I told Haggis.

'But he's got nothing to say!' spluttered Fiend.

'It's true,' Haggis admitted cheerfully. 'My brain is the size of a pea.'

To prove it, he shook his head from side to side. There was the sound of something tiny rattling around a large hollow space.

Haggis went on shaking his brain. The rattling sound actually had a kind of catchy, foot-tapping rhythm, like the *sh-ka-sh-ka* of a giant maraca.

Monsters in the Basement

I couldn't help picking up the beat.
Fiend and Norman were feeling it, too.
A second later, Norman had grabbed
his guitar – well, someone's guitar
– and was strumming along. Fiend
starting laying down some vocals:

'I've got EYES, baby,
I've got eyes.
You can't creep up on me.
Blink and move,
feel the groove,
Do the EYEBALL rap with me.'

Fiend might not have the most tuneful of voices, but he's a born performer. He was really getting into it – when the rattling sound suddenly stopped.

'Uh! Wait!' rumbled Haggis. 'I think my brain just fell out of my ear!'

Now that's an accident only a monster could have. Though I do sometimes feel that way myself in maths lessons.

I stepped towards Haggis to help him and heard a loud, squelchy noise from under my shoe. Er, I think I'd just found Haggis's brain.

I peeled it off the sole of my trainer and gave it back. 'I'm really sorry, Haggis.'

'It's no biggie,' he said happily. 'It's not like I was *using* it.'

Fiend and Norman nodded in agreement. Now that's friendship. How many humans would be that chilled out if you squashed their grey matter?

In-a-state Agent

One human who certainly wasn't chilled out right at that moment was the man from the estate agents. He had called round to collect the SOLD sign from in front of our house. He was talking to Dad at the front door.

'Mr Carlson, I . . . er . . .' The man kept looking nervously into the hallway. '. . . I've put the sign in the van. And here are your spare house keys.' He held out his hand. He was shaking a bit.

Dad took the keys, watching the estate agent suspiciously. He glanced at the golf club the man was holding in his other hand. He was clutching it a lot like you might hold a weapon.

'Expecting trouble?' asked Dad, nodding at the golf club.

'Oh, this?' The estate agent gave a forced laugh. 'Ha ha, no! Just, er, a big sports fan.' He took a practice swing with the club as if to prove it. 'Yeah, that's right. So, er, how are you settling in?'

'Great, great,' muttered Dad unconvincingly. 'This house . . . was it on the market long?'

The estate agent looked even more uncomfortable.

'Well, er, a few weeks, yeah.'

'Oh, yes? How many weeks?' pressed Dad. 'Just out of interest.'

'Two . . .' The man looked shifty. '. . . hundred and seventeen,' he finished.

Dad raised his eyebrows.

'Really? Two hundred and seventeen weeks. Do most houses take that long to sell?'

'Are you kidding?' replied the man. 'The good ones get snapped up like –' he clicked his fingers – 'that!'

'So why do you think it took so long to find a buyer for *this* house?'

'Oh. Well . . . er . . . I think your place has a lot more –' the man fished about for the right word – '*character.*'

'You noticed that, huh?' said Dad drily.

He suddenly remembered his manners.

'Do you want to come in?'

'Oh! No!' The estate agent looked horrified for a moment, then got a grip. 'Ahhh . . . places to go, people to see,' he said, backing away from the doorway quickly. 'Enjoy! You have a dream place!'

But the nervous look he gave over his shoulder as he hurried away down the drive, still clutching his golf club, didn't say 'dream'.

It said 'nightmare'.

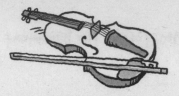

Norman's Plan

Norman made a weird noise.

'Norman has a plan,' Fiend told me.

Norman let out an odd squawking sound.

'He says, "let's tiptoe upstairs",' translated Fiend, '"crawl along the hall, sneak into the kitchen, find the sweetie jar and have away with the Lemon Bombshells!"'

'He said all that?' I asked. I was amazed one 'BLORKK!' noise could mean so much.

'Yes,' said Fiend. 'And he said, while we're up there, let's say "Hi" to your folks!'

'No!' It was my turn to squawk.
'You're not ready to meet them just yet!'
I pleaded. 'And I'm *certain* they're not
ready to meet you!'

All three of them looked upset. I'd
said the wrong thing again.

'I don't think you want to share your
family with us,' Haggis said sulkily.

'Yeah,' Fiend agreed. 'I think you
want to keep them all to yourself.'

Not true. If they'd met my mega-
annoying sister, they'd never have
thought that. But they were determined
to make me feel bad. Fiend started
laying it on with a shovel.

'We know when we're not wanted,'
he wailed. 'Perhaps you should just go
on upstairs and forget all about us.'

Norman produced a violin and began scraping out a sad tune.

'We'll just stay down here in some dark, dingy corner of the basement,' bawled Fiend, 'all on our lonesomes . . .'

He broke off to whisper to the others, 'Is he buying this?'

I wasn't. Not for a second. But poor old Haggis had tears rolling down his furry cheeks.

'I don't know,' he sobbed. 'But I am!'

I sighed to myself. It was time to strike a bargain.

Haggis Lets Rip

'OK – listen,' I said. 'One day soon, I promise, when my parents are in an all-time great mood, I'll figure out a way to introduce you.'

That put the smiles back on their monster faces.

'But for now,' I told them, 'you've got to be patient. And first you've got to prove to me that you can behave.'

'Anything!' beamed Fiend. 'Behaving is what we're all about! We're reformed characters now!'

I doubted that. A lot. But I had to give them a chance.

'OK. So let's try the silence thing again, shall we?'

This time, they really did give it everything they'd got. I was impressed. Even Fiend managed to keep it zipped for several seconds.

But gradually a rumbling noise started coming from Haggis's massive tummy. It began quietly and was followed by several ruder sounds from lower down. Nothing that impressive. I've done louder ones, to be honest. I bet you have, too.

But Haggis was getting more and more restless. He started shuffling from one foot to the other and making little anxious noises.

'Oh . . . oh . . . oh . . .!'

The tummy-rumbling was getting louder.

Fiend and Norman were watching Haggis with worried looks. Fiend suddenly cried, 'Uh-oh!' and the two of them dived behind the sofa. Next time, I'll know the warning signs, too.

'Why are you running?' I asked.

I got my answer a second later
– in the form of a thunderous, bone-
shaking, ear-splitting blast from
Haggis's *bottom*! He'd been spinning
about and somehow his massive
furry bum was aiming straight at
me! I got the full force of the violent
gust of monster wind, ughhh! I tried
desperately to stay on my feet as it
blew past me, making my
cheeks ripple and
my eyes water.
The force of it
landed me in
a chair and
then at last it
stopped.

The rumbling thunderclap had
shaken the whole house. Everyone
must have heard it – and felt it. I had a
horrible feeling Haggis had blown his
cover. Literally!

Sure enough, a moment later, I
heard Mum's voice yelling my name.

I tried to pull myself together. I needed to get up there, fast, and explain away the noise and tremors somehow.

I smoothed down my 'windswept' hair and hurried for the stairs – hoping I could smooth down the aftershock of Haggis's atomic bum-blast, too.

Aftershock

I walked into the kitchen, trying to look casual. My whole family was there. Dad was in full flow, firing frantic questions at Mum and Angela.

'Did you feel that?' he said. 'Are there earthquakes in England?' He was wide-eyed and talking in his high-pitched *What is going on?* voice. 'That was like five on the Richter scale!'

My sister was sniffing the air, looking puzzled.

'Can anyone smell lemons?' she said.

It was true. There was a definite hint of Lemon Bombshell in the air, thanks to Haggis.

Mum caught my eye.

'Are you OK, Eddie?'

'Yeah. Sure. What's all the fuss about?' I hadn't managed to think of a cover story so my plan was just to try and act like nothing had happened. Hardly genius, I know, but it was all I'd got.

Dad had gone to the window and was peering outside at the street. He turned back to Mum.

'The rest of the neighbourhood seems to be OK. Which means, whatever it was, it came from inside the house . . .'

Angela rolled her eyes.

'OK . . .' she muttered. 'If I was going to freak out, *now* would be the time.'

But Dad was already freaking out. He started pacing up and down nervously.

'We have to search the place!' he announced.

It was time for Mum to step in. 'Nick – you're overreacting,' she said. 'It's an old property. It's probably just some dry rot.'

Nice one, Mum. You could always count on her to come up with a sensible explanation. It was completely wrong, of course, but still . . .

Dad wasn't buying it.

'No!' he insisted, still looking crazy. 'I think we've got some really big *ghosts*!'

Mum raised her eyebrows. 'No,' she said firmly. 'I think you've got a really big *imagination*.'

She might have thought Dad was less crazy if she had seen what I could see. Dad's 'big ghosts' – Fiend, Haggis and Norman – were standing right outside the door into the hall. They were bouncing up and down like mad and waving their arms for me to join them.

Nightmare! What were they thinking?

Trying not to attract any attention, I moved over to the door and slipped out into the hall, closing the door behind me.

'What are you doing out of the basement?!' I hissed. I couldn't believe they'd come upstairs again so soon after our little chat.

Fiend didn't look the least bit sorry. 'We *need* those Lemon Bombshells!' he told me.

Norman honked his agreement.

'I mustn't let my blood sugar levels drop,' Haggis added. 'I get irritable!'

Can you believe them? They might be my best friends, but sometimes, I give up.

'Eddie?' shouted my dad from the kitchen. 'Is someone there?'

He must have heard us. If he found the monsters up here, it was all over.

'Hide!' I whispered, then ducked back into the kitchen.

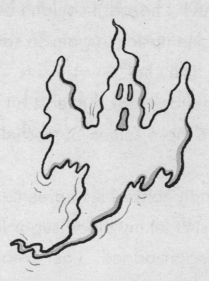

The Hunt Is On

Dad fixed me with a look.

'Eddie – who were you talking to?'

Time to think fast. If I made a joke of it, maybe I could throw him off the scent.

'Er . . . the really big ghosts?'

It worked, thank goodness. Dad scowled at me and turned back to his plan to search the house. He grabbed a handful of utensils from the kitchen worktop and began handing them round.

'Take this!' he said to Mum, thrusting one at her. 'You may need to defend yourself!'

Mum raised her eyebrows again. 'With a potato masher?'

But Dad wasn't going to be put off. 'Who knows what you're going to encounter!' he shrieked, waving a soup ladle.

Trust me, Dad, I thought, *you have no idea . . .*

Mum looked doubtfully at her masher. 'If I find something,' she

asked, 'should I boil it first?'

But Dad wasn't listening. Now that he had handed out weapons, he was ready to begin the ghost hunt.

I couldn't think of a way to put him off. I just hoped that the guys had found good hiding places.

'Eddie, come with me,' Dad ordered. 'Angela, go with your mother.'

He was acting like it was some sort of top-secret army operation. Sometimes, he is so embarrassing.

Mum frowned at him. 'What do you expect to find?'

Dad's face darkened and he lowered his voice.

'*Evil*,' he whispered.

Waving his ladle again, he signalled for me to lead the way into the hall. 'After you, Eddie.'

Nice, Dad. Real nice.

Hide and Shriek

Out in the hall, Dad silently waved me towards the stairs.

Rats. This wasn't good. Fiend, Haggis and Norman could have hidden anywhere. I had to warn them that Dad was on the prowl. I watched him start tiptoeing up the steps as quietly as he could.

'WHY ARE WE GOING UPSTAIRS?' I asked in a loud voice. Loud enough, I hoped, to tip off any large furry creatures hiding nearby.

Dad frowned at me and put a finger to his lips. 'Shhhhhhh!' he hissed.

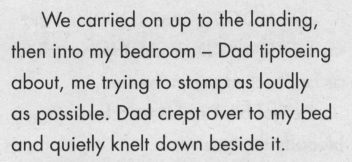

We carried on up to the landing, then into my bedroom – Dad tiptoeing about, me trying to stomp as loudly as possible. Dad crept over to my bed and quietly knelt down beside it.

'THERE'S NO POINT LOOKING UNDER THE BED!' I shouted. Haggis was way too huge to fit underneath, but Fiend or Norman could be hiding there.

Dad gave me another look.

'Why are you talking so loudly?'

'I'M NOT TALKING LOUDLY.' I did my best to look innocent, then watched as he checked under the bed.

He got back to his feet, frowning. Nobody there, phew.

I wondered how Mum and Angela were getting on downstairs. There'd been no yells or screams so far, which was a good sign. Maybe the guys had made it back to the basement after all.

Dad crept along the landing to his and Mum's room. He stood in the doorway for a moment or two, listening hard. Suddenly, his eyes widened. He jabbed a finger and mouthed to me as quietly as he could.

'I think there's something behind the door!'

Time to think fast again. Before Dad could move, I slipped past him and looked around behind the door. Then I reported back, shaking my head.

'It's all clear,' I told him calmly.

At least, I tried to look calm. In fact, my heart was thumping. Because the truth was that a giant furry orange monster was crammed behind the door trying not to move. Why had Haggis picked such a rubbish hiding place?

Dad wasn't convinced. 'I could've sworn I heard breathing,' he insisted.

I made a big show of checking behind the door again. Haggis had his eyes tight shut, and was bouncing up and down. But at least he was keeping nice and quiet. At both ends.

I turned back to Dad. 'Nope,' I confirmed as casually as I could. 'No one there.'

Just then, a deep, growly voice came from behind the door.

'Because when I close my eyeballs,' Haggis rumbled happily to himself, 'I am invisible!'

Dad stared at me in horror. He pushed past me into the room and peered nervously round the door.

You can probably guess what happened next. There was a split-second of shocked silence as Dad and Haggis got a good look at each other. Then, both of them let out long, wailing screams of terror.

Dad waved his ladle frantically. Haggis, terrified, tried to run. His massive furry body got wedged in the bedroom doorway for a moment before he squeezed through and fled, howling, along the landing.

I was just thinking that at least things couldn't get any worse when I heard Mum, downstairs, let out another blood-curdling scream. Moments later, Angela joined in with the shrieking.

That probably meant that they'd found Fiend and Norman.

That was it, then. The game was up. My Number One Secret wasn't secret any more.

Things Behind the Sofa

The next few minutes were total chaos.

There was a whole load of yelling, screaming and howling. Furry bodies and family members were running around the house, trying to get away from one another. I did my best to calm them down, but nobody was listening.

Somehow or other, Mum, Dad and Angela ended up cowering in the kitchen. Haggis, Fiend and Norman were hiding somewhere. I thought I'd seen Fiend duck behind the sofa.

And me? I was stuck in the middle, wondering which lot were daftest. And how to get them all to stop acting like loonies.

Dad was doing his best to play the brave hero. He was standing in front of Mum and Angela with his trusty soup ladle, ready to shield them from attack.

'Don't worry!' he said, wild-eyed. 'I'll protect you!'

This was getting ridiculous.

'There's nothing to be afraid of!' I told him. I led them into the living room and pointed at the monsters. Or at least at the sofa I thought they were hiding behind. 'These are my new friends.'

My sister nearly choked. '*Friends*?' She stared at me like I was insane.

'What kind of school do you go to?'
Dad wasn't happy either.

'Are you saying that you know
these . . . these . . . these . . .' He
struggled to find the right word. Fiend,
Haggis and Norman are hard to
classify. '. . . these things?'

'They may look strange,' I said, 'but
when you get to know them, they're not
really scary at all.'

'Hey!' came a voice from behind
the sofa. 'Who's not scary?' It was
Fiend, of course. 'I'm scary!'

'I've got horns!' said another voice,
this time from behind the door. That
had to be Haggis.

'Ohhh!' moaned Angela. 'This can't
be happening!'

It was time to sort this out. Someone had to take control.

I took a deep breath.

Meet the Family

'If you all keep calm,' I said. 'I'll introduce you.'

'Oh, this is so not happening,' muttered Angela.

I thought I might as well start with the bossiest monster.

'Fiend, come out and meet my family.'

Fiend didn't need asking twice. He took a quick peek over the back of the sofa with the small red periscope-like eye he has on the top of his head. Then he leapt up on to the sofa, grinning his crazy monster grin.

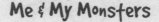

All three members of my family gasped and edged backwards. They stared at him, their eyes popping out almost as much as Fiend's.

'What is that?' wailed Mum.

'Urgh!' murmured Angela. 'Gross!'

Fiend didn't look bothered. In fact, he looked pretty pleased with himself. Like he does most of the time.

'And they said I wasn't scary!' he said, beaming. 'Aha! It's me! Fiend! That's right – feast your eyes! Ain't I a beauty?'

Dad was peering at him from behind his ladle. 'What . . . what . . . what are you?' he said.

'I'm a **monster!**' cried Fiend proudly.

Mum looked stunned. 'A real monster?'

'Oh, yeah!' replied Fiend. 'Totally. One hundred per cent.'

I thought it was time for my next guest.

'Haggis,' I called. 'Come out and say hello.'

There was silence for a few seconds. Then Haggis's nervous voice came from his hiding place.

'**No!**'

The big guy had
stage fright. Great.

'He's very shy,' I
explained to my family.
I tried again.

'Come on, Haggis!
Show yourself!'

Another pause. Then, very
slowly, Haggis shuffled into sight,
head down.

'Hello,' he rumbled awkwardly.
He gave Mum, Dad and Angela a little
wave with his massive hand.

They didn't reply. All three of them
were too busy staring, open-mouthed.
No surprises there. Seeing Haggis for
the first time is a bit of a jaw-dropper.
He's awesome.

'Look at the size of him!' whimpered Dad.

'I used to be afraid of spiders,' muttered Angela, unable to take her eyes off Haggis. 'But right now I *really* miss them!'

I thought it was probably best to press on.

'Norman!' I called. 'It's your turn. Norman!'

Norman must have decided to make his introduction a bit different. He has his own 'special' way of doing most things. He popped up out of nowhere, right next to Dad. Before Dad could react, Norman had thrown his furry purple arms round him and planted a great big slobbery kiss on Dad's cheek.

Dad pulled away, spluttering and wiping his face.

'Urgh!'

I made a mental note to talk to Norman about how to greet people for the first time. Not that it would do much good. Anyway, at least Norman had put a big smirk on my sister's face.

'Dad just smooched someone called Norman!' she grinned.

Haggis and Norman moved to stand beside Fiend, who was perched on the back of the sofa. Mum stared at the three of them.

'Where do you come from?' she asked.

I was about to explain, but Fiend

got in first, as usual.

'From a place far, faaar away,'
he replied, waving his arms in the air.
He made it sound like they were from
Mars or something.

My family all looked massively
relieved. 'Thank goodness for that!'
Dad sighed.

Trust Fiend to exaggerate. And, as
usual, I'd have to put things straight.
There was no point beating about the
bush.

'They live in our basement,' I said.

Dad's only response was a small
wail. Mum and Angela just stared at
me in shocked silence.

They definitely would have
preferred Mars.

Secret Passages

Now that Fiend, Haggis and Norman were out in the open, I figured it wouldn't hurt to show my folks their den. Looking back, I can see that this was probably a mistake. If you ever discover a monster den in your basement, my advice would be to wait a while before you give your family the full tour.

As it was, I had a tough time persuading Mum, Dad and Angela to go down there. But eventually, they agreed to visit the basement and take a look around.

I led them to the secret door in the hallway wall, which opens on to the basement stairs. As I swung it open, Dad gave Mum a puzzled glance.

'Did you come down here when we first viewed the house?'

Mum shook her head. 'I didn't even know it was here.'

Angela treated them to one of her extra-scornful looks.

'You're not very good at buying houses, are you?'

For Dad, discovering that the house he had bought had secret rooms and passages must have been the last straw.

'Right!' he said, digging in his pocket for his mobile phone. 'I'm calling the police!'

My heart sank. But Mum came to the rescue.

'And tell them what?' she said. 'That we've got *monsters* in the basement?'

Even Dad could see how bonkers that would sound. But he wasn't about to give up.

'OK. I'll call . . . Pest Control!'

'The mouse guy?' smirked Angela.

Dad looked desperate. 'Well . . . there must be *someone* I can call!'

I cringed as Fiend popped round the basement door, clutching a phone. 'I'll text you my number!' he offered cheerfully.

Angela's grin vanished. She was staring at Fiend's mobile.

'Hey!' she snapped. 'That's my phone!'

She wrestled it from his grip.

Fiend gave a 'Hmph!' and disappeared down into the basement. I set off after him, with the others right behind me. I heard Mum muttering as she followed.

'Eddie Carlson . . .'

When they use your full name, you know they're mad at you, don't you?

'. . . you are in so much trouble!'

Why? What had I done? It wasn't my fault *they* had managed to buy a house where someone – or something – was already living . . .

Down in the Den

The monsters were waiting to welcome my family as they came down the basement steps.

'Please – do come in!' cried Fiend. 'Where *are* our manners?'

Haggis, at his side, gave him a puzzled look.

'We don't have any,' he reminded Fiend.

That was another reason I loved hanging out with them.

Mum, Dad and Angela reached the foot of the staircase. I expected them to check out the rest of the basement. But they just stood there, gawping. They could not believe their eyes.

I suppose I've got used to it. But I can remember being as gobsmacked as them the first time I went down there. It's not like anywhere else I've ever seen.

Here's a picture, so you can get an idea what I mean:

'Would you look at this *place*!' murmured Dad.

'Cool, huh?' I said. Because as far as I'm concerned, it is. Totally cool.

'We didn't get an interior designer,' Fiend told them proudly. 'It's all us.'

'No kidding?' said Angela.

Mum was still looking around in awe. At least, I think it was awe. It might have been horror.

'Where did you get all this stuff?' she asked.

'Norman likes collecting things,' I explained.

At the mention of his name, Norman let out an enthusiastic **'RRRREEEP!'** He popped up from behind a box – with my dad's

underpants on. Good move, Norman –
NOT!

'Are they my underpants?' Dad
squawked.

'**FWEEESHT!**' went Norman.

Angela shook her head slowly.
'That's not a good look,' she told
Norman. She should have seen him
earlier.

Mum was the next to spot
something she recognized.

'Are those my pot plants?'

She didn't look at all happy to have
found them down here.

Haggis gave one of the plants
a gentle stroke. 'They're not very
talkative,' he sighed.

Mum just glared.

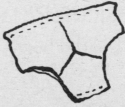

So far, this wasn't going as well as I'd hoped. I thought my family would be impressed with the monsters' den – that it might help them love Fiend, Haggis and Norman as much as I did. But it didn't seem to be working out that way.

And things were about to get a whole lot worse.

feel the Love

'IS THAT MY CAR?' howled Dad.

He hurried over to take a closer look. On the far side of the basement floor, there were a whole load of car parts that the monsters had 'found'. They had arranged the bits and pieces in the basic shape of a vehicle. It had four wheels, car seats, a steering wheel and everything.

'Yeah,' Fiend told Dad cheerfully. 'But we think it's broken. It doesn't *go* anywhere.'

Dad dropped to his knees beside the remains of his beloved car. I don't think he was keen on the remodelled version. In fact, he looked liked he might cry.

'What have they *done* to you, Speed Queen?' he wailed.

My sister got stroppy next. 'Are those my things?' she snapped. She'd spotted her missing hair-straighteners

and iPod – among other stuff – in a wicker basket right next to Norman. *Her* wicker basket.

Norman did his best to hide it. But
my sister is fast. She grabbed the basket
and started trying to wrestle it off him.
Norman gave a 'BRIL-LIL-LIL!' of
protest, but she just glared at him. And
Angela's glares can kill.

'*Trust me*,' she snarled, 'you
may be crazy, but you've got nothing
on me!'

Norman is a bit odd, I know.
Actually, make that a lot odd. But he's
not stupid. He let go of the basket.

Mum had spotted something else.
Another something that she'd been
missing. A whole stack of cookery
books. The ones she needed for her
work. Torn-out pages were scattered
around them.

'And I'll take those!' she growled, sweeping up the books and pages crossly.

Haggis looked devastated.

'But we haven't had pudding yet!' he wailed.

Dad had finally stopped crying over what was left of his car. He got up and marched over to Fiend, Haggis and Norman. He looked pretty fired up. I had a nasty sinking feeling.

'Right!' Dad yelled. 'I want everything back where you found it!'

Poor old Haggis obeyed instantly. He grabbed the nearest thing to hand. Unfortunately, it was Dad.

'Not me, you fool!'

Dad looked pretty funny, held up in the air by Haggis's hand, with his feet swinging off the ground. But I don't think he saw the funny side. And definitely not when Haggis dropped him. Haggis gets jumpy when people yell.

I could tell from Dad's face as he got up from the floor that he had had enough. He backed away towards the staircase, without taking his eyes off the monsters. Mum and Angela were a step ahead of him. All three of them began making their way back up the stairs.

'Listen – it's been great meeting you!' Fiend yelled after them. 'You're upstairs,

we're downstairs. Don't be strangers!
Drop by any time!'

Somehow, I didn't think my family
would be hurrying back. As a first
visit, it had more or less been a total
disaster.

But the guys clearly didn't think so.

'OK!' Fiend said cheerfully. He sat
on the sofa, with a job-well-done look
on his face. 'I think that went well!'

Haggis, too, seemed to think it
had been a great success. He flopped
down next to Fiend.

'Yeah!' he agreed. 'I'm feeling the
love!'

Norman gave a satisfied

'MMRRREEEPP-A-LoP!'

I didn't have the heart to tell them,

but I was pretty sure that love was the last emotion my parents or sister were feeling.

I made my way miserably upstairs, to face the music.

Choosing

It was all happening just the way I knew it would. The rest of my family couldn't deal with meeting Fiend, Haggis and Norman or their basement den. They'd freaked out, big time.

As soon as Dad got back upstairs, he was straight on the phone to the estate agent who'd sold us the house. Dad was determined to put it back on the market, so we could move somewhere else. Great.

But maybe there was still hope for Mum and Angela.

They'd come back up from the basement and Mum was making cups of tea to try and calm everyone down.

Fiend, Haggis and Norman came strolling into the kitchen and began looking at all the stuff in the room.

'That's my chair!' said Fiend, pointing at one of the kitchen chairs.

'Oooh!' said Haggis, waving a huge hand. 'And that one's my chair!'

Norman made a weird squeaking noise as he picked out his chair.

Fiend was already inspecting the things on the kitchen table. 'That's my plate!' he said.

Haggis went next. 'That's my –'

'Hey!' Mum interrupted. She gave the monsters a suspicious look. 'What are you doing?'

Fiend clearly thought this was obvious. '*Choosing*,' he explained.

Mum wasn't impressed. 'Oh, no, you're not!'

'Yes, we are,' insisted Fiend. 'We choose everything.'

'Not this time!' said Mum.

'We chose *you*,' mumbled Haggis.

Mum's face softened. 'You did?'

'Yeah,' Fiend agreed. 'Lots of families came to look around the house. We drove them all away with big scary noises.

'**BOOOGLY-WOOGLY-WOOGLY!!**'

'But we decided to keep *you*,' explained Haggis.

Angela raised her eyebrows. 'Wow! *This* family was the best you could do?'

Mum ignored her. She was busy listening to the monsters. 'How come you chose us?' she asked.

'Because when you came around,' said Fiend, 'you were always laughing!'

Even my sister couldn't think of a sarcastic response to this. Mum just smiled.

Unfortunately, Dad came in right then and he was looking even more grumpy.

'I've just spoken to our smarmy estate agent,' said Dad. 'When I said we'd like to put the house back on the market, he laughed at me down the phone.'

'So we're stuck here?' said Angela.

'Looks that way,' said Dad, frowning.

'Sorry, Dad-human-thingy,' said Haggis.

I couldn't help feeling a tiny bit hopeful. Maybe there was a chance I could keep the monsters after all? But the hopeful feeling didn't last too long.

Dad clapped his hands. 'Come on! Back to the basement!'

'I'm confused,' said Fiend. 'We thought Eddie was the boss?'

'*No*,' said Dad. 'He's the mini-boss. I'm the big bad grown-up version.'

'Shall we have a group hug now?' asked Haggis hopefully.

'GO!' shouted Dad.

This sent the monsters into a right state. Like I said, Haggis doesn't like being yelled at. He got a bit panicked and left through the dining room wall. And I do mean *through* it.

Me & My Monsters

Having a big Haggis-shaped hole in the wall didn't do anything to improve Dad's mood. Maybe being sent to my room wasn't such a bad thing.

The Deal

By the time my parents came up to
see me, Dad had managed to calm
down a bit. From the way they sat on
the end of my bed, smiling, I knew
they were about to tell me something
I wouldn't like.

'OK, Eddie,' said Dad. 'Here's
the deal. Look, the monsters have to
go . . .'

I knew it.

'. . . but in return, I am willing to
buy you that puppy you've always
wanted.'

'I don't want a puppy any more.'
Like that was even a zillionth as good
as three genuine monsters.

'How about a tortoise?' said Dad.
When I pulled a face, he tried again.
'A snake?' He wasn't one to give up.
'How about two snakes?'

'I don't want any of those things. I
just want the monsters.'

'Eddie, you have to try and
understand,' said Mum. 'Your dad has
this big new job, I have my career, plus
the house, and then there's you and
Angela to look after . . .'

I understood all that already. But I
couldn't see how any of it meant we
had to kick out Haggis, Fiend and
Norman. It was their home, too.

'We could spend more time together!' said Dad as if that would clinch it. 'I can be fun!'

'Can you juggle with your eyeballs?' I asked him. Fiend could.

'No,' Dad admitted. 'But I can do this . . .'

He pulled a rubbish face. Pathetic, honestly.

Mum took over again. 'It's for the best,' she told me. Grown-ups always say that about rotten stuff. 'I'm really sorry.'

'You made me leave behind all my friends in Australia,' I said, 'and now you want me to give up my only new friends. Don't you want me to be happy?'

They didn't say anything then. But it was too late. Nothing was going to make any difference. As far as they were concerned, the deal was done. The monsters had to go.

Goodbye, Monsters

'OK,' said Fiend tearfully. 'I guess this is it.'

He, Haggis and Norman were all gathered in the hall, by the front door, looking extremely glum. The whole family was there to see them off. I was feeling as miserable as the guys looked.

'We're all packed and ready to leave,' Fiend said emotionally. 'In a moment, we'll step through that door and out of your lives *forever*. I guess all that remains for us to say is . . .'

He threw himself at Dad's feet.

'...PLEASE LET US STAY!'

Haggis joined in. 'Oh, please, please, pleeeease let us stay!' he begged.

Norman was upset, too. He'd been using Dad's pants to dry his eyes. He

did a loud, snuffly nose-blow into them,
then passed them back to Dad.
Dad took the soggy Y-fronts
like they were toxic.

I couldn't bear seeing my friends so
upset. Or the idea that they were about
to leave *forever*.

Even my sister was finding it hard.

'This is awkward,' she muttered.

I could tell that she was already
starting to like having the monsters
around – however much she made out
otherwise.

You can't not like them. Hanging
out with them is always fantastic fun.
A bit chaotic maybe. Messy, definitely.
And usually pretty noisy and smelly,
too. But never dull.

And now Dad was going to send them away. The best friends I'd ever had. I'd never felt more miserable. I had to make him change his mind.

'Please, Dad?' I gave it one last shot. 'They've lived here practically forever. It's as much their house as it is ours.'

'Tell that to my bank manager,' muttered Dad.

'We'll try to be good!' Haggis promised. He was looking at Dad with big pleading eyes.

Norman honked his agreement. Fiend nodded, too, then added, 'Admittedly, it's an area we need to work on . . .'

But it was hopeless. I could tell Dad

wasn't going to budge.

'Don't make this any harder than it already is,' he said.

Do your parents use that line, too? It stinks, doesn't it? If it's that hard, why not just forget it?

Norman surprised us all by stepping forward and offering Dad his hand. Dad looked the most startled. But he took Norman's hand and shook it.

'Norman, that's very big of you,' he said, clearly impressed.

He was less impressed when he found he couldn't let go and that his hand was stuck to Norman's hand.

'Urgh! What is that? *Glue?*'

I had a feeling it was something much worse than glue.

It served Dad right, the big meany.
Norman obviously thought so, too,
from the way he was giggling.

'That's very childish,' Dad told him
crossly, trying unsuccessfully to get the
goo off his hand. He so wasn't
going to change his
mind now.

The guys must
have realized
this, too.
They picked
up their

belongings. Haggis let out a big sad monster sigh.

'Right then,' he said miserably. 'We'll be off.'

And with that, the three of them trooped out of the front door, heads hanging. Fiend was last to go. He closed the door behind them.

My sister gave Dad a hard stare. 'A real "feel good" moment,' she said sourly.

I was so angry and upset, all at the same time. It just wasn't fair.

'This family stinks!' I told my parents.

For once, Angela was on my side. 'How could you do that?' she asked Mum and Dad.

Mum looked pretty uncomfortable about what had just happened, too.

'It does seem a bit cruel . . .' she said to Dad.

A *bit cruel?* It was more than that! They'd just kicked three totally innocent monsters out on to the streets.

'The world is too big for them!' I yelled. 'They'll get lost. They can't survive on their own!'

But as it turned out, I needn't have
been quite so worried . . .

My New Improved Family

My family and I were still standing in the hall arguing, when suddenly there was the sound of a door closing. It sounded like someone had just come in through the back door of our house.

A second later, Fiend, Haggis and Norman came stomping towards us from the other end of the hall. They plonked down their stuff and let out contented sighs, as if they were happy to be home after a long journey.

'Wow!' cried Fiend. 'That was some crazy trip!'

Dad was gazing at the three of them in disbelief.

'What?' he said. 'All the way round to the back door?'

'It feels like we've been away for weeks!' cried Fiend.

I was SO glad to see them! I threw myself into a huddle with all three of them, giving my biggest and best hug. 'It's good to see you guys!'

'If I was going to say something nice,' said Angela quietly, smiling, 'I'd probably say it now.'

I broke away from our big monster huddle to have another go at persuading Dad. I was happy to grovel and beg, if there was even the tiniest chance . . .

'Can they stay just one more night?' I pleaded.

Mum looked at me, then at Fiend, Haggis and Norman, all watching hopefully. Then she looked at Dad.

'It *is* getting dark . . .' she said.

I could see signs of Dad beginning to weaken, I was sure.

'Can they, Dad?' I pressed, willing him to say yes.

He was squirming now, under
the gaze of six pairs of expectant
eyes. Actually, nine and a half,
if you count all of Fiend's.

'I'm almost certainly going to
live to regret this,' said Dad reluctantly,
'but . . .'

Say-yes-say-yes-say-yes!

Dad let out a sigh of defeat.

'OK.'

I went bonkers. Fiend, Haggis
and Norman went monster mad, too,
jumping up and down and cheering.
I'd never been happier.

'They can stay here on trial,' Dad
told me firmly, over Fiend's whoops,
Haggis's thumping feet and Norman's
triumphant yodelling. 'For one week

only. I'm putting you in charge of them,
Eddie.'

I nodded. I'd have agreed to
anything to keep them. Although I
doubted anyone could really be 'in
charge' of Fiend, Haggis and Norman.
You can't keep monsters under control.
They don't work like that.

In fact, I was pretty sure that one of
the cool things about having the three
of them living with us was going to be
that they made me look like a saint . . .

As if to prove my point, Haggis
suddenly decided he couldn't wait
to get back home to the basement.
Gasping with excitement, he turned
and charged headlong through the
door to the basement stairs.

Monsters in the Basement

Without opening it. Haggis style.

So that was how it all started.
Just like that, the Carlson family got a
whole lot bigger. Fiend, Haggis and
Norman got to stay in our basement.
And they weren't just my secret any
more – Mum, Dad and Angela were in
on it, too . . .

. . . And now you are as well.

So keep it under your hat, huh?

It all started with a Scarecrow.

Puffin is seventy years old.
Sounds ancient, doesn't it? But Puffin has never been
so lively. We're always on the lookout for the next big
idea, which is how it began all those years ago.

Penguin Books was a big idea from the mind of
a man called Allen Lane, who in 1935 invented
the quality paperback and changed the world.
**And from great Penguins, great Puffins grew,
changing the face of children's books forever.**

The first four Puffin Picture Books were hatched in 1940 and the
first Puffin story book featured a man with broomstick arms called
Worzel Gummidge. In 1967 Kaye Webb, Puffin Editor, started the
Puffin Club, promising to **'make children into readers'**.
She kept that promise and over 200,000 children became
devoted Puffineers through their quarterly instalments of
Puffin Post, which is now back for a new generation.

Many years from now, we hope you'll look back and
remember Puffin with a smile. **No matter what your age
or what you're into, there's a Puffin for everyone.**
The possibilities are endless, but one thing is for sure:
whether it's a picture book or a paperback, a sticker book
or a hardback, **if it's got that little Puffin
on it – it's bound to be good.**